Singularity

Singularity

Second Edition

Jayme A. Oliveira Filho and Jayme S. Alencar

Copyright 2021 © Jayme A. Oliveira Filho and Jayme S. Alencar.

Second Edition

All rights reserved. No part of this book may be reproduced in any form or by any electronic or mechanical means, including information storage and retrieval systems, without permission in writing from the publisher, except by reviewers, who may quote brief passages in a review.

ISBN: 978-1-956515-32-9 (Paperback Edition)
ISBN: 978-1-956515-33-6 (Hardcover Edition)
ISBN: 978-1-956515-31-2 (E-book Edition)

Library of Congress Control Number: 2021917785

Some characters and events in this book are fictitious. Any similarity to real persons, living or dead, is coincidental and not intended by the author.

Book Ordering Information

Phone Number: 315 288-7939 ext. 1000 or 347-901-4920
Email: info@globalsummithouse.com
Global Summit House
www.globalsummithouse.com

Printed in the United States of America

BOOK REVIEW

On a dying, late-21st-century Earth, a father and daughter discover transportation to distant space by means of black holes and seek to rescue a fragment of humanity via an evacuation ship. This debut from a father-and-son writing team is a short SF novel about a multigenerational team of space scientists trying to save the human race—or what's left of it. Deep into the 21st century, global warming and overpopulation are clear signs that the Earth has little time left to support life. In the United States, Joseph Silva, a brilliant astrophysicist from a devout Christian Brazilian immigrant family, while watching his daughter, Daisy, has a brainstorm about black holes leading to other universes. Anything strong enough to travel through the "singularity" of the black hole can traverse the cosmos and potentially locate Earthlike habitats. Daisy grows up to be a scientist herself. She works at NASA on projects to confirm her father's theories and make his dream a reality: finding a new world to colonize before humanity perishes. The God-given gift of a meteorite laden with the unknown metal alloy "Munerium" enables construction of extremely strong space probes and ships to survive the black hole's gravity. Daisy gives birth to a son, Alexander, who will be instrumental to the planned mission through the singularity in 2135.

—KIRKUS REVIEWS

Continue to page 72

CONTENTS

Dedication ix
Summary xi

Chapter 1: Hourglass 1
Chapter 2: The Impact 9
Chapter 3: Space Jump 17
Chapter 4: Into the Darkness 21
Chapter 5: Bittersweet 27
Chapter 6: Lunar International Space Station 33
Chapter 7: Frenemies 39
Chapter 8: The Selection 45
Chapter 9: Lunar Romance 49
Chapter 10: The Journey 55
Chapter 11: Decisions 61
Chapter 12: Canaan 69

DEDICATION

"THIS BOOK IS DEDICATED TO THE WOMAN, MEDICAL DOCTOR, MOTHER, AND WIFE: CRISTINA ALENCAR"

TAS=LYA

SUMMARY

The year 2020 has been a challenge for the whole mankind.

Wildfires, Storms, Drought, Death, Disease, COVID-19, Division, Violence, Social Injustice. This has been a tough year for all of us.

However, the night is darkest just before the Dawn.

SINGULARITY is a sci-fi book that focuses on the challenges that mankind will face during the 21st Century in special Global Warming. We will offer HOPE through human sacrifice, science, technology, faith, and imagination.

In the 1980s, scientists were warning us about the consequences of man-caused Global Warming and Climate Change. They warned us what could happen if we did not change our ways in the Future. Well, the FUTURE IS NOW. We are living the consequences of Global Warming.

We are breaking year after year the records for Warmer year ever recorded. Droughts are more common, which cause more extensive and devastating wildfires throughout the world. Storms are becoming more constant and causing more damage. Ice caps are melting, which are causing more coastal floods.

THIS IS CLIMATE CHANGE AT WORK.

In our book, we will see the effects that Climate Change caused to the Earth's Population and what mankind had to do to save itself from extinction.

We will use science, physics, action, love, romance, sacrifice, faith, and religion to explain this Humankind journey throughout the 21st Century to the beginning of the 22nd Century.

I hope you enjoy our SCI-FI.
(www.jaymeandjayme.com)
GOD BLESS.

CHAPTER ONE
HOURGLASS

In 2135, the indiscriminate use of natural resources and atmospheric pollution left the world in disarray. Unscrupulous twenty-first-century politicians disregarded the scientific community's warnings, and now the world is succumbing to its own greed. Wild climates with torrential storms, dust bowls, flooding, drought, rising oceans, and coastal cities are disappearing. The world's population is in panic mode. States are crumbling as people watch their lives come down to nothing. All hope vanished; the world desperately needs a savior, but who would step forth and raise a helping hand? What will it take to reverse all the damage to the ecosphere? The desperate cries of the world are unmistakable. Yet, the thought of changing the destinies of earth's inhabitants' corrosive behaviors is unthinkable.

There's always an answer for everything happening under the sun - all humanity's hope rests on the shoulders of a young man and his crew as they try to find a new home. Alexander, an exceptionally talented young man, and natural leader was an excellent recruit for the International Space Command Center (ISCC). Here he met up with his love in a unique environment. He uses science and his faith to become a wise leader. His family motto is "God's Blessings and Hard Work." He has this engraved on a bracelet given to him by his mother, Daisy.

Alexander always lives by the family motto. He is also a devout Catholic, just like his great grandparents. As Alexander looks at a sandstorm forming over the horizon where once a flourishing forest covered the landscape, he remembers his great grandfather and the gift that could change people's future. His great-grandparents were immigrants from Brazil. They came to the United States to further their studies. His great grandmother was a medical doctor, and his great grandfather was a dentist. They had just one son - Joseph.

Joseph was born in Brazil, the son of the proud Silva family, and immigrated to America. He was so proud of both heritages that he always worked hard and took every opportunity given to him for success. Joseph loved the mystery of the universe; when he was eight years old, he received a gift from his father, changing his life and future an hourglass with the inscription, "Time is Relative. Brilliance is Not. From Darkness to Light." The beginning of the twenty-first century was a period of many uncertainties in the world. Scientists were discussing the rapid increase of pollution in the atmosphere with the accumulation of CO_2. The building-up of greenhouse gases began raising the temperature to the point of no return for the Earth. Scientists were giving their warnings, but politicians were not listening. This was when Joseph received this gift from his dad. Although concerned about the world's future, he was also optimistic about the ingenuity of the human spirit.

Joseph grew up to realize his childhood dream of becoming an astrophysicist. But he never forgot the gift his dad gave him and the meaningful inscription. By the time Joseph finished his education, the worldwide weather had become more unpredictable, with more prolonged droughts and stronger storms. In fact, he overheard two elderly people in a discussion which piqued his interest. As he passed by an old shop in his area, Joseph noticed the elders were engaged in a friendly conversation.

"It never used to be this long without the rain," the woman said before the other gentleman replied, clad in an old, grey suit, "Yes, causing so many droughts around the world. In the last two years, the droughts have increased. This is insane!"

Drought, huh? Joseph's curiosity made him stop and eavesdrop on the elderly couple like when he was a child. So, his thoughts had been correct; the droughts were more frequent, and something must have happened that caused all these shifts in the climate. But global warming destroyed the atmosphere, and humans could no longer stay silent; drastic action needed to happen, and Joseph was excited to find a solution.

He was trying to elaborate on a new theory about space and time. He studied the old and current concepts of astronomy and physics but became fascinated by the start of everything–the big bang.

When thinking about the start of everything, it involved life and matter. The state that the universe started from massive and unimaginable pressure and gravity. It concentrated all the matter in the universe on a point known as a singularity. Joseph could never cope with the idea of everything coming from nothing. So, he tried to devise a new theory explaining the old paradigm of "everything coming from nothing."

The technology of singularity in today's world is tech driven. Looking at it from this angle, they define singularity as "the hypothesis created an artificial super intelligence will trigger a huge technological growth, resulting in unfathomable changes to human civilization." These changes speak of many creations that are to come out of this intelligence. For example, the big bang could have resulted in creating the universe, including its many features and life, a tech-driven big bang - with humans at the center of it all - resulting in creations benefiting humans at large.

Joseph was a brilliant young man, recognized by his peers and colleagues as a man of expertise and wit. He was an immense fan of Albert Einstein, who revolutionized science at the start of the twentieth century with his relativity theory and many thought experiments (an experiment carried out only in the imagination). Einstein was the first to create the idea of the universe not being just a space. Still, everything correlated and interconnected through a medium called the "space-time fabric" (fabric in which objects of the universe embed themselves), a new concept Einstein used to explain gravity's interaction of mass distorting the surrounding fabric. The distortion creates the orbits, just like the gravity wells (gravity wells result from the pull of gravity caused by a body in space such as a planet) in science museums. Using a coin for this concept is like throwing it inside a well. Following the curvature of the well, the coins go until it falls to the bottom. The coin following the well's wall illustrates the distortion objects with a significant mass cause in the space-time fabric. The distortion promotes the movement of planets around the sun. These gravitational waves were first detected and identified, proving Einstein's theory in 2016.

Joseph adored thought experiments and the concepts of the space-time fabric established by Einstein. He imagined situations in his head to solve complex problems. In one of his thought experiments, he created a new theory revolutionizing the science world and reshaping the future of astrophysics.

Besides being an astrophysicist, Joseph was also a father of a young girl named Daisy. One day, he took Daisy to a park, and she went to jump on a trampoline. He saw his lovely daughter jumping up and down on the trampoline, going higher and higher. Unfortunately, the trampoline fabric was being distorted as she landed on it.

His mind exploded into one of his thought experiments. What if his daughter kept jumping on the trampoline until she would stretch the fabric to a point in which they could not pull her back any longer? What would happen? Would she fall to the ground? His mind became wild with many imaginative ways to prevent the distortion and apply it to his thought experiment. Therefore, he imagined his daughter would keep distorting the fabric until, at a point, she would move to another place, another dimension, another universe. He started thinking. What type of distortions would affect the universe enough to design a kind of fabric stretch throughout space? What was so massive that it could distort the fabric of space-time to the point of collapse?

The solution came to him like a bag of rocks slamming against his head–a black hole (a region of space-time where gravity is so strong that nothing—no particles or even electromagnetic radiation such as light—can escape from it); from this point of extreme gravity in the universe where light can escape, there's an immense pull. Here, the black hole would squeeze all the matter into a singularity (a location where the quantities used to measure the gravitational field become infinite in a way that does not depend on the coordinate system). The big bang started with a singularity, and black holes ended in a singularity. Could there be a connection to both? At this moment, he remembered the gift his father gave him when he was eight years old. The hourglass inscribed with the saying, "From Darkness to Light." Joseph wonders whether the "nothing" came from "something?" Like an hourglass, the matter could flow from one space to another. Perhaps a vast black hole would distort and disrupt the fabric of space-time to the point of rupture? Then, it would transfer all the matter absorbed by a black hole to another universe through a big bang event, "From Darkness to Light," "From Black Hole to Singularity."

In a single instant, his mind was open to the vastness of the universe. He was floating in the middle of the Milky Way Galaxy, looking straight into a monster black hole, a star called Sagittarius. Inside singularity's black hole, through a tunnel being funneled to another singularity, a wormhole to a brand-new big bang universe. He could see his thought experiment on his mind. The cosmos became a multiverse with many galaxies interacting with each other through destruction and creation. When he awoke from his reverie, feeling like an eternity had passed, Daisy was still jumping on the trampoline, ignorant of the ground-breaking theory he just envisioned. She had become part of the beginning, part of history, playing a valuable role guaranteeing she would prove his father's theory in the future. Yet, she continued to jump, with no cares, enjoying her day.

"Dad?" When she spoke his name, the visions of galaxies dissipated, and all he saw was a tired daughter.

"Hey, Dad, can we go home? I'm done." She smiled, and his heart melted.

"Let's go; I can tell you've had enough for today. I am tired as well."

She gave out a short, contagious laugh and just smiled, "I like it when you have to admit you get tired!" He looked to see a smile flicker across her face, showing gaps from the inevitable loss of teeth to the Tooth Fairy.

"So, you like it when I am tired?" he said.

"No, I didn't think you ever became tired. You are always moving and thinking."

"That may be true, but I'm older, and I don't need as much sleep. However, sweetheart, when you are tired, it means you have been exercising, which is always good for your body but remember you must sleep well to rest both the body and the mind–especially when you're little."

"Whatever!" She smiled back at him. Joseph smiled at her too, but his mind became caught up in a world of black holes. Understanding the process, Joseph knew he had an enormous task in front of him. The ground-breaking work ahead of him would take a lifetime, but success was the only option.

Joseph's battle was to complete the puzzle in his mind. But in science, sometimes the puzzle gets completed long after the trials. So, rather than bringing the equation straight to writing, it takes time. Conceiving, researching, hypothesizing, theorizing, and putting all the calculations into a comprehensive theory.

As Daisy and Joseph journeyed back home, the time seemed short. Joseph considered the voyage he was about to embark on would take him away from his daughter. But, knowing the personal struggle and sacrifice which needed to be made, Joseph always knew his choice. In the end, the world had to be saved, and although Daisy might not understand now, in the future, she will embrace his mission and sacrifice, knowing he did this for her and humanity.

CHAPTER TWO
THE IMPACT

Joseph started working on his theory. He had big questions to answer - what if the universe is inside a black hole and the dark energy continues to expand? Would the universe's matter absorb into the black hole into another universe? Would singularity be the same type as in the big bang, and can they connect it to a wormhole?

Therefore, he started working on his theory. He had a big question that he had to answer. What if our universe is inside a black hole and the dark energy that continues to expand our universe is matter being constantly absorbed by this black hole from another universe? Therefore, the singularity of the above-mentioned black hole would be the singularity of our Big-Bang. Both singularities would be connected by a wormhole.

The wormhole solved the Einstein field equations for gravity. It acts the same as "tunnels" by connecting the points in space and time. Thus, wormholes could allow space travelers to take a trip between two points (say, Earth and Mars) and complete the journey as quickly as traveling to outer space.

This concept of an expanding universe was proved and established by the famous twentieth-century astronomer Edwin Hubble in 1929, where he found the universe was not static but expanding. More recent analyses have shown this rate of expansion speeding up.

Expanding the universe is like someone blowing a balloon. The balloon would get larger and larger until no more air or matter is available. Thus, the rate of expansion would be the rate of the balloon being blown.

So, Joseph continued working hard developing his mathematical formulas to begin his procedures:

- Expansion Rate = Velocity Rate of Matter being sucked by the black hole. (ER = BHMv).

- Black hole matter = visible matter + dark matter + dark energy. (BHM=VM+DM+DE).

SINGULARITY

- Black Hole & Big Bang (B.H. & B.B.)

By calculating the exact size of a black hole, he could create an alternative universe with this new equation, {Black hole size = Space/Time (13.7billion years) + visible matter + dark matter + dark energy} [BHs=S/T+VM+DM+DE]. The solution to Earth's increased heat, drought, and insect outbreaks, all linked to climate change, are just the start of the calamity wreaking havoc on the world. Essential daily needs will evaporate; declining water supplies, reduced agricultural yields, health effects in cities due to heat, flooding, and erosion in coastal areas would put Earth at the brink of extinction. But if this formula could come to fruition, it may save Earth's people.

Overjoyed by the hope this formula could work, Joseph continued to exact all the needed information. He knew the method would work whether the data gets lost inside a black hole. Knowing the work of Antoine Lavoisier, the man who determined oxygen was the fundamental substance in combustion, and then named the element. He established the law of conservation of mass, decided that combustion and respiration caused by chemical reactions with oxygen (www.sciencehistory.org / historical-profile/antoine-laurent-lavoisie) proved black holes transferred data to other universes but did not absorb them. Therefore, Joseph also believed, nothing leaves in nature by transforming everything from chemical elements to entire galaxies. Instead, a new black hole would create an alternative universe and transform matter into a new big bang in this light.

He thought, "Is this crazy? Is it that logical and straightforward? How am I going to prove this outlandish idea? Does multiverse (an imaginary collection of diverse visible universes, each of which would include everything available by a linked community of spectators) theory explains what I'm trying to create?"

Indeed, proving these things will be tricky, especially when figuring out how to translate one's mind to paper and the people. The process must be seamless, and people must understand the underlying crisis, respond well to the research, and execute the transition. The proven science allows the world to know everything presented to them will work - this theory will inspire the world. However, understanding the task will be insurmountable, and most of the work would take years before its completion. Joseph hoped he would get the chance to face the world and let them know how much he sacrificed to save the world. Joseph was beginning a colossal undertaking and intended to succeed in every way. His only motivation and his "creation" will revolutionize how the world envisions space travel.

Initially, the process began on a rocky path; progression was difficult for him. He became the joke of the science community, ridiculed, and ostracized by the same colleagues and institutions that one day would applaud him for his achievements in astrophysics. The battle raged on for a prolonged time, but he never doubted himself or his work. Although sometimes he wished he had help from other scientists and his determination waned, all he had to do was think of his daughter's laughter as she flew on the trampoline that faithful day, inspiring her dad to do great things.

Daisy was a small child when her father, Joseph, experienced his thought experiment while playing on a trampoline. Years after that faithful day, Daisy has spent many hours alone, with her thoughts. She always wondered what would have happened if she was playing on the swings or jungle bars? Would her dad have developed the same formula and had the same extraordinary life? One will never know, but one thing was true: she adored her father and would do anything to help him. As a result, her dad devoted his life to attempting to prove his theory. Most professionals in the science community rebuked his work, but his work was not unnoticed by some people closest to him, including his daughter. So, it's not surprising how much he had influenced his daughter. She saw how passionate Joseph was about the universe and how much work he put into everything the challenge presented. When any discussions about the project whispered into Daisy's ear, she always made herself present. Her countless hours spent in Joseph's lab learning anything to help her grow into the articulate person getting ready for college. When the time came for her to leave for college, at sixteen, she went to the best engineering school in the United States, the Massachusetts Institute of Technology (MIT) in Cambridge, Massachusetts. As part of their engineering school, students can achieve specialty ranks in aerospace, aeronautical, and astronautical engineering (all ranked number one in the nation). MIT piqued Daisy's interest, and in the end, there was no question about which college her application was going to be mailed to - MIT.

Daisy spent five years getting a Ph.D. in Aerospace Engineering. NASA recruited her out of school. After spending years at NASA working on various successful projects, they honored Daisy with the appointment of Associate Administrator of Aeronautics Research and were in a place to help her dad prove his theory.

The project's controversial ideas alienated Joseph from society after his friends and contemporaries deserted him. Scientists in prominent positions in aerospace engineering destroyed his reputation and his ability to find funding. Joseph knew the consequences of a vision, and he never faltered from his project. But Daisy knew dreams required protections, and she would fight to ensure this project would continue through NASA with herself in charge. Daisy stood resolute in propelling the project forward. She noticed her father showing signs of weariness, and she just couldn't let his dream die. Joseph was a tough man, but people can take only so much embarrassment, especially in front of his wife and kids. Somehow, he ignored all their hateful words and stayed convicted to achieve his life's ambition.

Daisy looked forward to working with her dad. They were so close; Daisy would speak to her dad every day. She would ask her dad why he continued to pursue his theory with so many critics.

He would tell her, "Let no one tell you what you have to do. Believe in something and fight for it to the end."

With determination in his eyes, Daisy could see his soul when he said, "One day, I will prove the theory a success. I believe in this. I will keep trying and practicing my theory because you know…" and she would repeat, "practice makes perfect." So, they both keep trying, kept practicing, and hoping one day everything would fall into place. But in this case, the practicing part was taking too long.

Years and years passed with little headway. Joseph persevered with determination, inspired by the most influential scientist in his life, Albert Einstein. Whenever Joseph needed a self-confirmation, he would focus on Einstein's spirit "I think and think for months and years. Ninety-nine times, the conclusion is false. The hundredth time I am right." Joseph then continued to push on, knowing one day, he would save the planet. Although most of the malcontents and disparagers gave up spewing their loathing and moved on to another poor soul, Joseph knew that he needed to execute his vision. Failure at this point would be a monumental loss and a story people will never forget. He just did not want to be in the history books for the wrong reasons. His daughter supported him—it made it sweet like icing on the cake, even if the dream took time to realize.

Daisy knew it was time for her to become involved in the day-to-day practices of the project. Her primary role was checking in, sending her dad messages, and ensuring his budget was right. Now, her attention will be on progressing the project to the end. She didn't want to act like politicians who support ventures, only to never keep their promises.

Knowing something impressive needed to happen with this project, she met with the entire NASA aerospace research team and her dad. They decided the only way her dad's dream will stay alive would be to send a probe inside a black hole and collect the data from inside. As always, this was an impossible task. First, Sagittarius was thousands of light-years away, in the middle of the Milky Way Galaxy. More precisely, 26,000 light-years (a light-year is the distance a beam of light travels in a single Earth year). Second, a computer capable of sending information from inside the black hole back to NASA was necessary.no probe could enter a black hole without being destroyed by the immense gravity.

The solution seems more complicated than wormhole traveling. But now, the team had a precise plan, one Daisy could use for her knowledge and specialty. So, she started developing a probe capable of traveling into a black hole and survives the immense gravity that would crush any standard probe. First, she tried metal alloys to find the right combination to support the tremendous gravity, but all samples failed. Every time her frustration started getting overwhelming, Daisy remembered her father's saying, "practice makes perfect." So, the test continued.

Joseph was getting old, and Daisy was afraid her dad would never see his theory proved. She had the design and concept for the probe, but she could not solve the three problems, distance, information, and resistance. But then, on the morning of August 15, 2071, a sudden opportunity was about to present itself and change the trajectory of Joseph's dream.

Daisy and her team, a year ago, started seeing signs of an asteroid getting close to the Milky Way Galaxy. Their first calculation showed the meteor passing Earth with a generous margin of distance. However, as it hurled closer, it moved closer, bringing it within one-fourth the distance to the moon. Finally, the team readjusted their original findings and reported the meteor would strike Earth in the Sahara Desert at a monstrous speed.

As the scientists waited for impact, they gave reports daily to ensure the public wouldn't panic. Knowing the meteor will hit Earth's atmosphere, the entire world focused their research on the meteorite on the planet. Soon scientists realized this was no ordinary meteor. As the meteorite hit, the impact crater was immense, yet it did not fragment as expected. Once the scientists arrived at the impact site allowing entrance to the meteorite, they analyzed and observed that the "rock" was not a rock. Made from a metal alloy never seen before, the scientist did not classify the object. After months of discussions and debates, the scientists held a press conference, releasing their findings to the public. Extensive investigations and research conducted in the laboratory left little clues to the origins of the meteorite. They concluded this was a new metal alloy, which they named Munerium.

Daisy was at her house, having her breakfast when she glanced at the TV to see a news conference. She thought that the meteor could be the missing piece for her probe. If the meteorite could be intact after such an unbelievable collision, maybe the metal alloy would be strong enough to support the immense gravity of a black hole.

She contacted the research team, who discovered the rock, and asked for a sample for her studies. They told her "No." She then began submitting documentation and data on the wormholes and the probe, showing this project's importance for humanity. But again, it was a "No." She made a few more phone calls and contacted her NASA friends. Within a week, she had a piece of Munerium for her studies. She was on her way now.

She started studying the alloy, and she could not believe it. The alloy could withstand the tests of enormous gravitational pressure.

"Eureka!" she exclaimed. "I found my missing piece!"

Now she would need help to solve the other two puzzle questions – quantum computer and nuclear gravitational propulsion engine. She put her faith in the stars, knowing the answer would provide help soon.

CHAPTER THREE
SPACE JUMP

A meteorite with an unknown origin, made of Munerium, imploded into Earth. Most scientists divide meteorites into three main types: stony, iron, and stony iron, each with many sub-groups. Stony meteorites comprise minerals that contain silicates - silicon and oxygen. This extraordinary material, with the fantastic quality, which gets more potent when submitted to immense pressure and gravity, would be perfect for this project. Munerium adapted to stress and outperformed any known substance on Earth. The behavior of the Munerium led the researchers to hypothesize that the atoms forming the material would transform into a crystalline structure, indestructible. When tested under infinite pressure and gravity—not one buckles, distortion, or bend.

People believe the meteorite hitting Earth was a sign for the end of all times, but the reality of the impact was a miracle—a shot in the dark gift. They sent the material from the heavens to give hope and save humanity one day. Many people could not look past the asteroid's devastating impact; a tiny few believed it was an omen of worse things to come. Yet, millions of people knew the beacon of light when they saw it and these icons from industry: science, education, medicine, business, and so many more insisted the world step up and help the nation get back on track.

When the Munerium meteorite fell into the middle of the Sahara Desert, it created a massive media rush and overwhelming fear among society. The media blew the entire incident out of proportion with their over-zealous reports on comets, meteorites, asteroids, and don't forget, meteors. But the truth is the teams won the lotto with this meteorite. Meteorites do not come from comets, which are more fragile than asteroids; ninety to ninety-five percent of meteors fizzle out before they reach Earth's atmosphere. The Munerium meteorite beat the odds of being in the ten to five percent of making it through Earth's atmosphere without falling apart. As Munerium plummeted to Earth, it remained intact; not a single piece broke off. Something so important just dropped on the scientists' doorstep was, without a doubt, a miracle.

People knew asteroids falling from the sky would break into several fragments because of the impact of Earth. However, if one were to measure the weight of an average asteroid falling from the sky, the weight would increase as gravity became a factor. This is because Munerium did not break up.

Munerium's crash into Earth was a miracle. As soon as the meteorite hit, the National Security Administration (NSA) scientists rushed in taking control of all the information and analysis gathering. But after months of being no closer to a conclusion and overwhelmed by a plethora of data, the scientists were left with massive unanswered questions with no answers in sight. One of their first mistakes was not organizing teams, experts, and specialists to process the data dump. So the first call they should have contacted was Daisy. She would have sorted through all the information swiftly. But, more importantly, she was the most notable meteoriticist in the world. One of her specialties known throughout the aerospace community was her work deciphering and identifying the compounds of stars, asteroids, comets, and meteors. Eventually, the NSA decided it was time to regroup and bring in the experts.

The rescue call from NSA came while Daisy and the team strategized and waited for their turn at the meteorite sight. At this point, it could be months before ever seeing the rock. Daisy looked up from the meeting when she heard her secure line ring.

"Daisy, there is someone on the line for you." Said Daisy's assistant, Marlene, handing her boss the phone.

Daisy looked at Marlene quizzically, knowing nobody calls on that line unless it was essential. But it was this simple call that changed her life and the entirety of her teams. A chance for a new discovery — a life devoted to honoring her dad. She couldn't believe the Project Director at NSA wanted to speak with her about traveling to the Sahara Desert. But there was no question of them going, and trip details were planned. Within a month, the team, Marlene, and Daisy were off to their next adventure.

Scientists are, by nature, optimistic; they believe in continuing their path when most people give up. Daisy was passionate, as her road started years before, and she had to do this for her dad. Some tasks people embark on are enormous and maybe without optimism, especially if someone is trying to prove the hypothesis of a parent's lifelong dream. Daisy was not that person; she came from a family whose whole life was optimistic; regardless of the outcome, Daisy would always know she did the best she could.

A giant hole formed when the Munerium meteorite affected the earth. Her first observation of the Munerium was it never broke into pieces. The meteorite's strength must have a complex schematic giving it the ability to resistant the forces of atmospheric pressures. Daisy needed to fabricate vast amounts of Munerium necessary to build a giant spaceship; so, the teams worked to create a synthetic Munerium.

Then Daisy had an earth-shattering idea; she found a connection between the oxygen isotope inside Munerium and the Moon. The characteristic of the lunar oxygen isotopes comprised oxygen, silicon, magnesium, iron, calcium, and aluminum. Daisy calculated it would find the most potent isotopes in the dead volcanoes and craters. Would a synthetic Munerium be strong enough to withstand the crushing power of a black hole? The oxygen isotopes in rocks on the moon may be identical or have homogeneous features as those on Earth. However, recent studies revealed the earthly and lunar oxygen isotopes were not as similar as thought. Although the isotopes may not be identical to the lunar isotopes, they will work well with Munerium making plenty for the spaceship. The chemical composition of the lunar rocks makes it possible that isotopes can withstand enormous amounts of pressure. But now, she needed to develop collecting the raw materials and then injecting the oxygen isotopes inside the Munerium.

CHAPTER FOUR
INTO THE DARKNESS

In 2074, two scientists engaged in a friendly competition to see which one would have the most relevant invention of the decade. Professor Christine was developing the first quantum computer. Quantum computers based on the theory of quantum physics and quantum mechanics use the quantum entanglement property, which states that when two objects or particles are in contact, they remain connected forever regardless of the distance. Therefore, the ability to connect with information between unimaginable points in the universe or different universes would propel electronic technology far into the future.

Developing this computer took decades; trial after trial frustrated the scientists until that faithful day, it showed promise. Researchers will put so much of their life into their projects. No one wants to put their name or reputation on the line, only to fail. Then a kernel of an idea explodes into the ultimate vision researchers have poured into their souls. They are just waiting to give flight to their dream. Prof. Christine was one such researcher; she was in the latter stages of decoding, adjusting the last details of the motherboard to be operational.

Quantum entanglement brings forth a deeper understanding of the several worlds of quantum theory. Quantum entanglement is that quantum theory requires multiple worlds to exist or function. And when there is quantum entanglement, the two worlds are not independent of each other. Choosing Mars to test Joseph's theory is convenient as NASA had just landed the Mars Perseverance rover. Through human negligence and climate change damaging the Earth year after year, choosing Earth was obvious. These two worlds are not independent of each other as Earth and Mars are hexagons (just examples); this creates a linking relationship — or positive correlation in statistics.

Then, Professor Heart developed a new type of propulsion called the Ionic Nuclear Graviton Engine (INGE). This new propulsion system would distort the space-time fabric and create a wormhole, a shortcut through space-time. Per his calculations, he could decrease a journey of 1,000 light-years to less than an Earth's hour. As Einstein proposed in the past, "time is relative." A person flying in space has a different time count and perspective than someone on Earth. This is because of gravity and his general relativity theory.

Gravity is a vital phenomenon representing everything with mass or energy pulled together or brought toward another. When someone jumps, it is gravity that takes a person back down to the earth. In space, when humans go there, it's like tossing ashes into the air - they take time just flying around above the surface as they have no significant weight. When people travel in space, their experiences may differ because gravity is relative; time perception depends on the observer.

Professor Heart had a straightforward explanation for his theory. Imagine a sheet of paper, and on that sheet of paper, there's a point in each extremity. Regular physics believes the smaller distance between two points is a straight line, but one could make the two ends connect by bending the paper in half. Thus, creating a shortcut between two points in space by generating a wormhole; he called this a space jump.

Professors Heart and Christine were impressive scientists, and they were running against time. Earth continued to be ravished by climate change; coupled with human activity, Earth has sustained irreversible damage. Moreover, resources are dwindling at a faster rate, challenging the allocation to every person. This alone justifies the scientists' urgency for a breakthrough into another world.

While prodigious minds are busy with their inventions in 2074, the weather on Earth had reached a tipping point because of extreme deforestation and farming or construction on wetlands, to name just a few. The skeptics believed something was about to happen to the planet. Coastal cities were being flooded, droughts were becoming more severe, storms had become more robust than ever, crises were being triggered in many countries, and millions were dying every year from the effects of climate change - The Runaway Greenhouse Effect. Scholars were not optimistic about the future of humanity on Earth. The weather patterns achieved positive feedback in a vicious cycle and became more and more hostile to the world population. Everybody was looking toward the skies for a new possible, livable planet or moon to sustain Earth's population.

Earth's twin, Venus, billions of years ago, experienced the exact destructive climate change as Earth. Venus' atmosphere destroyed by harmful greenhouse gases like carbon dioxide caused its water bodies to evaporate, making it unbearable for life. The interior of Venus, made of a metallic iron core, comprises a molten rocky mantle. While on Earth, human activity and manufacturing industries killed the planet by releasing tremendous amounts of CO2 into the atmosphere.

Therefore, it was imperative to have both Professor Christine's and Professor Heart's concepts proven so a suitable location for human colonization might begin. A glimmer of hope sparkled when both professors announced they had finished their missions and was ready to test them. First, however, both professors needed a spaceship strong enough to support the astronomical gravitational fluctuations involved in this experiment. Not having their own vessel, the innovators contacted the one person who might help them, Daisy.

They had heard about her tests with Munerium and her thoughts on the development of a space probe. So, when the professors called Daisy, she was ecstatic to hear about the prospect of testing Joseph's theory of black holes and alternative universes. But the professors had other ideas. They did not want to send a probe to Sagittarius; instead, they wanted to test the space jump and the quantum computer concepts to see if they would work. Daisy was adamant she needed to use the probe she designed after the first tests for Professors Heart and Cristina were successful.

This is how it should be in life - people embracing the power of negotiation. After all, life revolves around using what's at one's disposal. Scientists sought collaborative projects to benefit the masses; for a solution to saving Earth's inhabitants, all three teams - Daisy and the two professors - needed to stay united to the end.

With a compromise reached, everyone went on to create history. About to launch the engine-computer-probe, the trifecta team expected success. The scientists decided the first test would be in an empty Milky Way Galaxy, 1,000 light/years away from Earth. The probe should take only one hour in space-time but one year on Earth time. When successfully tested, the probe will be sent out to make inquiries of the Sagittarius star.

They set a date for the test on September 22, 2075. The weight of humanity hung on their shoulders. The teams watched as the rocket left the Earth, carrying the probe out of space. Daisy held her breath, waiting for any sign of trouble. Scrutinizing every part of the rocket for a deformation, bend, or buckle, then it happened. Without fanfare, the rocket released the probe. The Ionic Nuclear Graviton Engine was the first to fire and kick in, and the quantum computer began making calculations. But it was the probe that brought the most excitement when it created a distortion in the space-time fabric and formed a wormhole constructed. The probe will take one Earth year to transmit any data back to NASA. The only thing for the team to do now was hope and prays the probe reached the correct location.

Waiting over the past year was the most stressful for all the team members. They had no proof that the probe survived; did it disintegrate as soon as it entered the wormhole?

One year mark of the launch arrived. Each person from all the teams gathered in mission control, awaiting any sign of life. After a day of waiting, there was only silence and a quiet murmur of dejected voices. Again, instead of the control room silence throughout mission control; still no sound of "computer life." The longer the silence loomed, the more nervous everybody became, but it was Professor Christine who broke the silence, "we will hear from the probe, and we will be successful. In fact, we should receive data from the probe within the next few hours."

They waited and waited - hours became days, and days became weeks until weeks became a month. Dismayed, Professors Christine and Heart did not know what happened. Maybe the probe was not strong enough, the quantum computer did not work, or perhaps the space jump was unsuccessful? They questioned every aspect of their projects and mission. Yet, Daisy would not admit defeat, knowing what she had built. Instead, she told them, "I know it will work, no doubt at all." She had developed this patience from the years she when started her father's groundbreaking theory.

Just at the point of no return and complete failure, the sound everybody has been waiting to hear—printers buzzing, monitor screens turning on, and the sigh of relief from the trifecta team. Putting all one's faith in a probe took gumption, yet in the end, good news will always prevail; all one needs to do is believe. Finally, after thirty-two days of waiting, the quantum computer sent a signal saying the ship reached the destination and all the instruments were working well and in perfect condition. Mission control exploded in celebration when seeing this news. They had pulled it off — they had pulled the impossible off.

Professors Christine and Heart could not contain themselves, but Daisy was quite pleased by the news but still not satisfied. Instead, her thoughts were with Joseph. How much he endured, how much ridicule and mockery thought to be the laughingstock of the scientific community. He told the world about the possibilities of black holes and the big bangs; now she has the chance to prove to the world that everything her father communicated to them was right – she will not squander this opportunity.

CHAPTER FIVE
BITTERSWEET

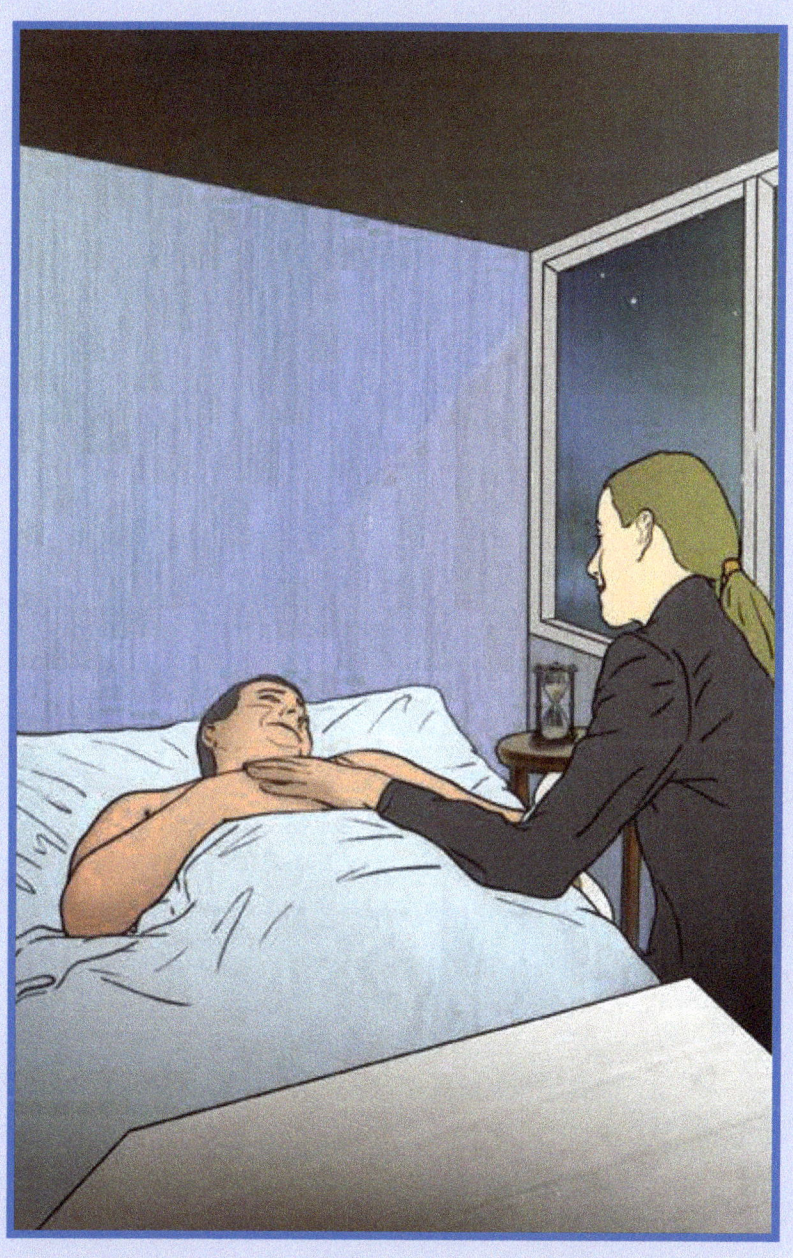

Allen and Carr, the two probes Daisy designed and fabricated with the remaining Munerium, were on their way to be hurled through the black hole right in the middle of the Milky Way Galaxy, Sagittarius. Each probe contained 200 space drones equipped with an ionic engine and quantum computer, all designed to search for a new universe, seeking signs to prove Joseph's theory of traveling through a black hole to squeeze all the matter into a singularity and arrive in another universe.

A conventional rocket will blast Allen and *Carr* into orbit. Once released, the ionic engine and quantum computer instantly engage. The journey should take 26 hours, but 26 years will pass for the researchers before they know their success. Einstein's theory of relativity of time explains how time passes depending on a reference time frame. According to someone in a different frame of reference, the faster a clock moves, the slower time passes.

Now the waiting game would start. Daisy and her father would have to wait 26 years to see if his theory would save the world. She could only hope her dad would still be alive to experience his contribution to humanity.

Waiting for a year or two to receive the answers to one's dream must seem like a lifetime, but to wait 26 years was an eternity. Daisy's father was up in age, but he had to live long enough to realize his dream. Daisy had plenty of work to do, but the space control center was still a lonely place. Waiting a lifetime was unbearable.

Daisy, up for another sleepless night, was wandering around her kitchen when the phone rang. Jumping at the abrupt intrusion, she picked up the phone. It was her assistant, Marlene.

Marlene said, "Daisy, you need to come to the control center."

Daisy asked, "What happened?"

Marlene replied, "Allen started transmitting data."

Daisy said, "What? How is that possible?! The probes transmitted data only outside the wormhole." And that is precisely what happened.

Allen's ionic engine failed midway through the journey toward the Milky Way Galaxy. Then, the quantum computer started transmitting info, and Daisy detected a problem in the engine ventilation system, making it overheat and stop working. Daisy was distraught at the thought of everything ending; she just couldn't tell her father.

All hope now rested on *Carr*'s shoulders to survive the journey and the encounter with Sagittarius; unfortunately, the wait took 13 years. Meanwhile, the team worked tirelessly analyzing the details on the engine transmitted by Allen. They needed to understand the failures and not replicate them in the next probe.

Carr entered the massive black hole in the middle of the galaxy, where everybody's anticipation tingled every day that passed by without a sound. The air tensed inside the space control center. The anxiety was palpable, and Daisy could barely control herself. Waiting for any signal from the probe gnawed away at all the team members' confidence. Yet, the wait continued, and the entire members of mission control waited, waited, and waited.

Again, right at the brink of failure, the probe started transmitting. The control room exploded in celebration. *Carr* had survived the journey, and it was about to plunge inside the black hole. According to Daisy's calculations, the probe should suffer the spaghettification process with the compression at fifty percent of its volume and a stretch of 4 times its length. Hopefully, her calculations were correct, and the probe would survive the unimaginable gravity of the black hole.

The probe should travel quickly inside the black hole, but again, it stopped transmitting. Daisy's team all had the same thoughts, was the probe destroyed, or did it survive and go through the singularity of the black hole to an alternative universe.

Days and days passed with no signs of a transmission. Daisy felt destroyed; everything the teams worked so hard to invent may indeed bring nothing, as well as the proof of her dad's theory. In her head, her dad said, "Rise up, keep your head in the game. I have given you the ability to always feel hopeful, feel faithfulness. I never taught you to quit, don't start now." She perked up, deciding to check-in at mission control. Walking in, she noticed an indicator light was blinking on the monitor; she stopped breathing for a moment. *Carr* was transmitting.

Carr was sending info from an alternative universe. Tears streaming down her face; she then knew her dad was right all this time. He was right.

Daisy started running diagnostics; it had survived, damaged but intact. Just half of the space drones were available and operational for deployment and exploration of this alternative universe. This was important because the drones would start searching this new universe for a habitable planet. The mission is to prove her dad's theory and look for a new home for humanity. So, they sent the space probes.

Working with Professor Christine and Professor Heart was an imaginable joy that filled Daisy's heart. This was a day she rejoiced with them and remembered all the team's hard work to prove her father's theory. She found the answers.

Barely containing herself, she rushed into her father's house with a mixture of accomplishment and closure. However, the most joyous moment can turn into a nightmare in a second. Lying on the floor, Joseph was not breathing and on the verge of death's bed. Daisy quickly called for an ambulance and started CPR. She finally felt a pulse, but she did not know how long he was on the floor. Finally, the EMTs arrived and started life support procedures. They were off to the hospital before she thought about what happened.

As she drove to the hospital, she couldn't believe such a jubilant moment could turn into such a devastating situation. Seeing her dad lying on the floor was not the scene she was expecting or expecting. Racing into the emergency room, she found her dad. Now, her father was crashing, and the doctors were doing everything they could to save him. Her first thought was that he had to survive long enough to tell him about the probes. Now, the tears started forming, both for the exhilaration of the achievement and the reality of a dying father. This was the man full of energy, never stopping, giving all his inexplicable power to prove his theory.

Watching parents grow old is difficult; the sight is even more painful when a parent, full of life, becomes ravaged by sickness. But the child can still see the twinkle of their childhood in their parent's eyes; it's only their bodies failing them in the end.

Joseph was in critical condition, and Daisy watched the doctors try to stabilize him. All Daisy wanted was a minute with her father; his theory was correct, and he was about to save the world. Finally, the doctors allowed her to speak to her dad. He was so weak, but he absolutely understood what Daisy was telling him. It thrilled him to have such excellent results, and he could leave Earth knowing he would save millions of people.

Daisy and her dad both cried because they knew this was the last conversation they would have. Amid their celebration, Joseph still faced death. But for him, it was a blessing to hear that his theory will shake the foundation of space travel.

Daisy said to her dad, "You were right, Papa. All this time, you were right. You made the biggest discovery of the century. Your theory will go down in the history books as the greatest achievement of ALL time!"

Mustering the quietest whisper, "You, my beloved daughter, are my greatest achievement. What you became will be my legacy."

Daisy sensed he needed to know nothing would have been achieved had it not been for his initial work all those years back. She also told him that whatever career she would do later in her life was because of Joseph's ideas and work. Of course, Joseph wanted to give Daisy all the credit, but it was his to relish.

After Daisy's speech about how the project was all his work, a smile broke his face; delighted, she smiled back. As for Joseph, he looked sideways as the smile on his face broke into a concerned countenance. He knew his time had come. He struggled to look at his daughter, knowing their celebration was over; Daisy knew too.

In the end, his heart gave out before his love for life. He looked back to her and said, "Please take the hourglass and this necklace with the crucifix on it." Daisy's world started spinning around her; she felt her heart freezing.

"Don't leave me alone. I can't do this without you", said Daisy, in between her sobs. Right before he passed, he heard his daughter's sad words. He looked up, smiled, and blew her a kiss, his way of saying, "You'll be fine." Daisy would have to believe her dad and know in her heart she can never be alone with her father's love inside her soul. Sadly, Daisy sat down beside him as tears trickled down her cheeks with no words coming out of her mouth. After some time, she burst out crying, and it came out so uncontrollably, and she was inconsolable.

An extravagant burial ceremony for an exceptional individual, Joseph Silva, exalting his kind, optimistic, and faithful life. Then, finally, the entire group of mourners touted his life's work and diligent sacrifice to save the Earth. The celebration went well into the night; everybody knew his absence would profoundly affect their lives, but so many of the people celebrating his life were project team members, and they knew the effort they were making would go into the history books in his honor.

Ultimately, Daisy needed to go back to her daily routine, with one exception, no trip to her dad. However, she will always be proud of how history will surely remember Joseph's groundbreaking contribution to Earth's continuation. As for Daisy, finding Joseph's journals and other treasured items from his closet, the crucifix necklace, and the hourglass helped her feel closer to her dad. One day she will pass these memories on to any children she might have, a memento of their granddad, a great pioneer in astrophysics who valued perseverance and determination throughout his life.

CHAPTER SIX
LUNAR INTERNATIONAL SPACE STATION

After a few months off, Daisy threw herself right back into work on the project, *Knight Discoverer*. With any luck, one of the space drones from *Carr*'s journey would make its way through the black hole and would start sending data. Time was of the essence.

Daisy was working night and day on the *Knight Discoverer* project. Her whole life never gave her the luxury of meeting someone, saying it would only interfere with her work. However, she was really depressed and emotionally frail after her dad's passing. So, she started seeing a psychiatrist help her through the unfinished business with her father. In due course, Daisy began feeling like her old self and started living her life again.

Through her many years at NASA, Daisy has seen many engineers come and go on her projects. Yet not one of them ever sparked any love interest, until one day she met a new NASA research aerospace engineer, Tom Avanco, when he joined her team. He was an experienced engineer assigned to Daisy's team to help her with this gigantic project. The connection between the two of them was apparent from the beginning. The two of them became fast friends, leading to confidants and finally lovers. Although they were both older, it was not an issue for either of them. Daisy could not wait to be part of a relationship, something she had never experienced. Already in her fifties, Daisy knew having a child would be impossibility. The Earth was dying, just another reason not to have a child. However, God has his own plans for people. Nothing would stop them, so enjoy the ride.

Daisy continued designing the *Knight Discoverer* while waiting for the space drones released by *Carr* to send any type of info back to the mission center. Tensions were growing as everyone realized the project, they were working on was all for nothing.

Daisy had not been feeling well for about two weeks. She was lethargic and had occasional nausea. Tom told her to have it checked out. The two of them went to a medical office at NASA where she explained her symptoms, had an examination, and finally some blood work. When the doctor entered the exam room, she had a smile on her face. Daisy was confused; obviously, it couldn't be bad news. Finally, the doctor just couldn't contain herself, and she blurted out, "you're pregnant!"

Daisy and Tom stared at her for what seemed like an eternity. Then, finally, she spoke, "I cannot believe this; how did this happen?!"

The doctor tilted her head to Daisy, "I think you know the answer to that question."

Shocked, Tom looked at Daisy. "This is the happiest day of my life. But, of course, getting married to you is number one too."

The emotions came flowing in, and she started crying for both happiness and sadness. She was happy because her family legacy would continue, but now she will bring a child into a dying world, which caused her much pain.

With this mixed emotion fogging up her head, Tom and Daisy walked back to the car. They were both stunned, but they were both ecstatic, knowing their love had created a human being just for them. Everything was going all right. However, Daisy understood the drones needed to make contact; otherwise, she just contributed a life bound for extinction.

Startled by the ringing of her phone, Tom answered, "hello?"

"Daisy?" said Marlene, her assistant.

"Hold on, she's right here," he handed Daisy the phone, as she quietly said, "What's up, Marlene?"

"What's wrong? Something's wrong. Are you okay? Did the doctor give you some bad news?

Daisy looked at Tom to see if he thought it would be okay to tell Marlene about the baby. He smiled and nodded, "yes."

"No, there's no bad news, only good news–no–spectacular news. I am pregnant. Tom and I just came out of the doctor's office. I will have a child."

Marlene started screaming and exclaimed, "I am so happy for you! Congrats! This couldn't have happened on a better day."

"What? What's happened? Why did you call me?" Daisy said with concern.

Marlene replied with excitement, "I will tell you that the news is unbelievable. You're just not going to believe it."

Daisy, confused, replied, "What?????? Tell me."

Marlene settled down and said, "Are you sitting, and are you calm? This is HUUUUUUUUUUUUUGE!"

Daisy replied, "I am in my car, so yes am sitting. Tell me already!"

Marlene exclaimed, "We found it! We found it!"

Daisy, curious and confused with the conversation, replied, "Found what????????????"

Marlene started crying.

Marlene, filled with excitement and all the emotions all at once, replied, "One of the space drones started transmitting data from a solar system. This is a dual solar system, and one planet is in the habitable zone and has an atmosphere and gases like Earth and liquid water on its surface! So, we found Earth 2.0.!"

Daisy and Tom started hugging, and then Daisy cried. A ton of weight on her shoulders floated away after carrying it around for thirty years; her teams had accomplished the impossible. Marlene, still on the phone, was screaming and crying with happiness.

New earth, a new beginning for humanity. Another miracle.

Daisy, still hugging Tom, calmed down and replied, "This morning, I had no hope for the future of our child, and now there's nothing to hold our child back. Thank you, Lord. You are a miracle worker."

They name the new earth *Canaan* and the two stars orbiting *Canaan,* called *AFDATA* and JSA.

The only logical next step was taking a trip to the Moon and constructing a lunar base for isotope collections. Although the construction of the Moon lunar base was not quick, the team had all the information required, including the tools to be used. Daisy received daily reports on the station's development. Working at NASA was a great asset, making the monitoring of the progress easier. Ultimately, the completed base started sending isotopes to Daisy's lab. Now, with the production line regularly collecting and shipping back isotopes, Daisy began the next step.

Sending the ship was next on the list; Daisy had an idea to help put the ship into the black hole for information without being torn apart by the immense gravitational pressure inside the black hole. Daisy went full force on this project. The quantities she needed for the build were enormous; gratefully, the harvesting of the oxygen isotopes, forming a synthetic Munerium, was moving along well.

Daisy drove her team just as hard to ensure the vessel sent was strong enough to resist spaghettification (this is the vertical stretching and horizontal compression of objects into long thin shapes (like spaghetti) in a non-homogeneous solid gravitational field) (https://en.wikipedia.org) when it enters the black hole. Again, the Information gathered and this new discovery, Munerium, played an essential role in the probes and rocket's design. Pursuing this design approach would give the ship a better chance of surviving the pressure inside the black hole known for consuming or sending away everything near it in its powerful gravitational pull.

Destroying probes was not an option at this point; they had accumulated enough knowledge to ensure someone built the probes well equipped before they left Earth. It thrilled the scientists involved to execute their first mission. But, just like before, everybody worried. How would this really work? Although everything checked out, the probes and *Knight Discoverer* could contract and condense its atoms as the volume decreases by fifty percent, while the length will stretch to four times the original size. With the ship extended this severely, the fear of all mission scientists rose. One minor element breaking or misfiring, and years of work are up in smoke. The only bright star in this first run of *Knight Discoverer* comes from the knowledge Munerium is the only substance known in the universe capable of resisting the immense pressure and gravity of a black hole. The expectation of success from around the world rested on one rocket.

CHAPTER SEVEN
FRENEMIES

With so much clamoring at work, Daisy never seemed to have enough time to luxuriate in being pregnant. Yet, when she did find those moments, they were so special. Rocking in the chair, Tom drove all the up to Vermont to pick up from a special artesian he had always admired. Her hopes and joys are all bundled up in the round belly she rubbed. When Tom and she went to get their first ultrasound, Daisy just cried. This child really was a miracle meant to conquer the world. Every time Tom and her went for check-ups, it still was overwhelming to see and hear a life growing inside her.

Daisy was having a restless night; she thought maybe the contractions were starting. She would wake Tom when they grew closer. Eventually, she briefly fell asleep until an electrical shock went through her body. Daisy awoke in unbearable pain, focusing her pain on the sun making its first announcement to the world.

"Tom, Tom … I think I'm having a …. contraction, the pain … won't go away." She barely could get the words out.

Tom jumped out of bed, turning on the lights. As soon as he saw the blood in the bed, he knew they had a problem. He called 911 instantly and then went to Daisy and tried to comfort her. Unfortunately, by the time the E.M.T.s arrived, she was racked with pain and about to pass out.

Tom was beside him, "This is not the way the delivery was supposed to go. But, oh Lord, please protect the two people who mean more to me than anything in this world."

He jumped in the car and followed the ambulance to the hospital. Entering the E.R. was chaos. A team of doctors and nurses were huddled around Daisy, preparing her for surgery. As Tom approached, a nurse escorted him to the waiting room. Once there, she collected all of Daisy's medical information and informed him they took her to surgery as they spoke.

Tom shrank, "What's wrong? What's going on?"

"She has a tear in the amniotic sac, and the doctors are going to do a cesarean section immediately." The nurse told him.

"Can I see her? I can't have anything happen to the two of them." By now, Tom was on the verge of tears.

"Of course, this was one of the reasons I came to see you. We need to get you gowned up so you can see your new baby. Let's go quickly; the baby is not going to wait." She said with a smile on her face.

Whisked off the surgery room, Tom was finally joined back with Daisy. She looked so tired, so scared, and yet so excited. The following words Tom heard were, "Okay, dad, it's about time to see your new baby."

Tom went behind the screen and saw his baby coming. It was the most exhilarating moment in his life. Words cannot be spoken to explain the brilliance of birth. Quickly, the doctor had the baby out, and Tom cut him an umbilical cord; it was a boy. The doctors continued working on Daisy to ensure the rupture was resolved and there was no additional damage.

The baby was whipped away to get the medical attention he needed. Tom returned to Daisy, waiting for the first cry of their son. Yet, there was no sound, still nothing, nothing, nothing! Tom rushed around to the baby, and they were giving him C.P.R. to revive him. Tom couldn't believe what he was seeing. He just saw his baby boy born, and there's no way he's not coming home to his family. Then, in a second, the sweet sound of a wail was music. Tom ran back to Daisy and watched as the nurses handed her the baby, Alexander.

Daisy and Tom had nothing more important in their lives than seeing their son grow up with as much love and support parents can give. He was adored, and they spent all their time with him. All the attention paid off for Alexander; he was a curious and quizzical child. He loved spending his spare time at NASA with his mom and dad. Just like his mother, who was also a "lab rat" when she was young, he just couldn't stay away. He watched his mom and dad go through their days, working on pieces of the shuttle, analyzing data, and sitting in on meetings now or then. Eventually, he would become an astronaut; Alexander knew he would be dazzled and dismayed by this career forever.

Alex was a young man, but he was different than the kids his age, who liked spending their days being fascinated by newly released movies, fashion, and girls. He had the maturity of a wise old man and his parents' work ethic, plus the legacy of Joseph's perseverance, the family's secret of success. His years in preparation for his future, amid the stars. Early in his life, he earned his grandfather's crucifix, which he used to make difficult decisions; Alexander would hold the crucifix around his neck and say this prayer, "Give me the wisdom and knowledge I need to make this decision. Make me follow your will. Amen." He knew he would always be protected; his legacy never let down.

Growing up, Alexander was brought up in the Christian faith. Though his parents' jobs were extremely demanding, they never stood in the way of the observances and writings of God. Every Sunday was a day of worship, and the family seldom missed. Their after-church ritual meant a lunch of lively debate about life, space, school, or anything else on their minds. Alexander's parents loved each other intensely; he would watch the way they spoke to each other, so knowledgeable, bright, and full of wonder in their eyes. His parents always looked at him the same way, making him feel full of love. He knew his path in life was to make the Silva family history wealthier; stopping wasn't an issue.

When Alex had his tenth birthday, his mother gave him the Silva legacy's most precious gifts. His great-grandfather had passed them down to his only son Joseph, his grandfather, and Joseph passed them down to his only child, his mom. Now my mother was passing them down to Alexander, her only child. The Silva legacy, an hourglass with the inscription, "Time is Relative. Brilliance was Not. From Darkness Into Light," was an anthem to the character of everyone in the family; one Alex pledged to often. However, what she did next, Alex never forgot; she had created her own legacy piece for him to pass down to his children along with the others. It was a gold bracelet with the family motto inscribed, "God's Blessing and Hard Work." She was now entrusting him to keep all the values, ideals, and determination given to him by both his parents and to become the best person possible.

Many people in the aeronautics field knew his family well and would have been more than happy to give him the upper hand, but it wasn't an option. He always worked hard and never stopped. Alexander's track for success may have been paved by the difficult times of his grandfather and mom, but Alex could not rest on his laurels. Joseph started his dream with no more than an idea, a concept with few people believing in him, barely any resources or people to help. Alexander hated when his mother told him how people ridiculed his granddad, saying his ideas would never be proven. For him, it sounded like it was just yesterday, and he felt like it was his responsibility to work harder to keep proving to people how far someone will go to achieve their dream.

On many occasions, when his parents would work late, they would come home and find him in the kitchen cooking. If mom seemed too tired, he would also do the dishes. His family was always about having each other's back, and he did not take this lightly; he will continue to support his future children in the same way. Plus, he will always seek the guidance of life from the Lord.

The years quickly flew by; of course, he was on track to graduate from high school early, just like his mom did, and go to college. He knew his mother was a graduate of M.I.T., but he wanted to go to the school with the most graduated astronauts - United States Air Force Academy in Colorado. Although he was excited, his mother was apprehensive as she remembered her time at M.I.T. as a young person. So, when he was sixteen, Daisy and Alexander packed up what he needed for the academy and stuffed the last of the boxes into his dad's car. Daisy wanted to go on the trip to Colorado, but Tom and Alexander felt it would give them the extra time they needed to bond. Plus, Tom had graduated from the academy, and he was so proud he couldn't wait to provide Alexander with the exclusive tour.

Alexander walked over to his mom, and he felt just for a moment driving away was impossible. But his mom smiled her beautiful smile, and he knew everything was going to be okay. Final good-byes said as Daisy stood in the middle of the street as the car drove off, watching her future and the world's future fade out over the horizon.

CHAPTER EIGHT
THE SELECTION

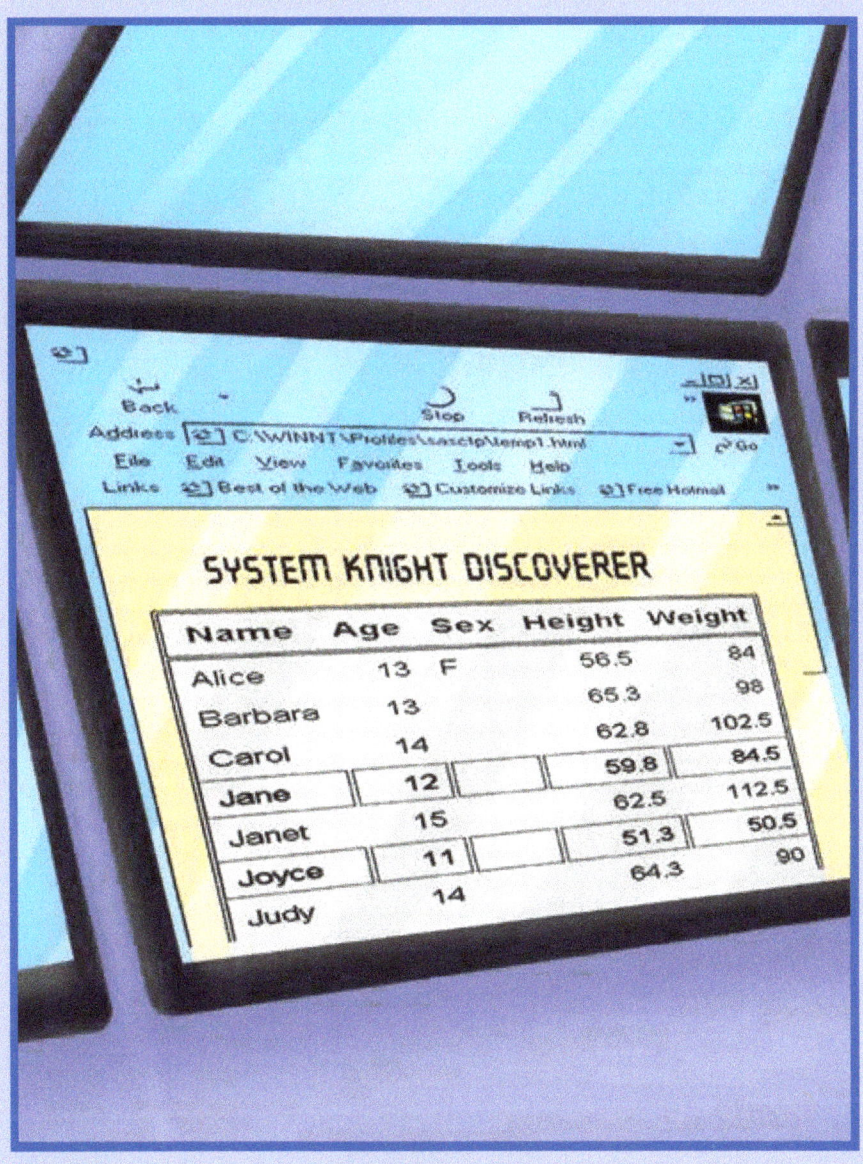

Now it was time to make the hard choices; all the accolades had been heard, but now it was time for reality.

Clearly, everybody wanted to survive the apocalypse and go to *Canaan,* a typical survival instinct as soon as society knew the spaceship would be launched in the next few years. However, the fear in people's eyes, trying desperately to find a way on the craft, began to grow more feral as every year passed. So driven to board the ship by any means necessary was the mission of billions of people. Most people had nothing left in their lives except to create elaborate plans to sneak into NASA and enter the spaceship.

NASA had become a militarized zone bunkered down. At the beginning of the twentieth year of the ship development, the entire mission control facility and all the team and crew members and their families were moved to a forty-story bunker underground to protect them. Once the selectees from the lottery are established, they too will be housed in the bunker.

The most crucial strategy of protecting the spaceship was moving it and its construction crews to the Lunar Station. Then, not only will it be easier to have quality control over the ship, but there would also be a slim possibility of anybody hijacking the rocket.

Finally, a committee of twenty people from across the world was randomly chosen by Presidents and leaders of all countries. The team represented all walks of life, but not all countries. For the selection to work, the committee members were anonymous to each other (they sat with chaperones worldwide in secrecy), and none of the team members would be selected for the journey.

Hopefully, with the world's people on board with a system, there would be fewer challenges about those who will be selected. However, the committee was optimistic at best; the world was in a frenzy. Nevertheless, a lottery system was eventually agreed upon by members without much fuss. It was the next step, the criteria of who will be placed in the lottery in which chaos ensued. The group themselves seldom went through a session without heated discussions – as they were deciding which 9.9 billion people would die on a dead Earth while 22,000 people flew off into space to a new, better planet.

Their selection process needed to be wholly defined and absolutely with no room for compromise; no matter one's wealth, influence, power, or connections, the lottery selectees will not change once they come from the computer.

Hot debates set the tone for the first meeting as each member tried to present their own agenda. One consensus heard throughout the hall was how to determine the age of the elderly left behind. Some members wanted the cut-off point at seventy years old. Who would be there for them without relatives and no one to protect them? But, on the other hand, some committee members argued people below seventy could be productive on the new planet since there are chores to be completed in people's homes.

As the arguments continued, the elderly number went down to sixty until the members eventually settled for the cut-off age of fifty. This final decision was the first to condemn millions to death at the hands of a toxic planet.

It was the following conversation everyone was hoping to avoid, but each member agreed to be thoughtful and logical no matter the reality of their heartbreaking decision. It was time for the cutoff for the youngest. The panel discovered there were still too many young people to put in the lottery. The young adults in the lottery needed to be industrious, childbearing, productive, and healthy. Again, the criteria used for deciding the future of the youth needed to be critical. Argument, after argument, the team finally decided twenty years or older would be placed in the lottery; the room was silent. How sad to end a day knowing only twenty thousand people had an opportunity to save humankind, and this committee decided the fate of the 9.9 billion people left behind.

Once the lottery committee's criteria were posted on social media, people felt it was not fair to vote for life and death decisions, primarily if it was motivated by the need to provide workers on another Earth. However, people were outraged when the masses emerged with the knowledge that the young adults were needed for more than work, their ability to bear more children for colonization of the new world.

The ship's limitation was twenty-two thousand people; two thousand reserved for the International Space Command Center's crew members comprised scientists, engineers, technicians, military personnel, command crew, and families. The next 20,000 people would come from the lottery. The lottery placed names of all the inhabitants of Earth between the ages of 20 and 50 went into a computer system where 10,000 males and 10,000 females were randomly selected to colonize the new world, *Canaan*. The spacecraft team would take care of all passengers, ensuring their safety. This mission, vital to the colonization of *Canaan*, was the last hope of humanity surviving extinction.

Everyone was selected for the trip to *Canaan*, just for *Knight Discoverer* to be completed and ready for launch in 2135.

CHAPTER NINE
LUNAR ROMANCE

As time passed, residents of the Earth were facing a bleak future —something had to be done as soon as possible. As such, Alexander was selected as one of the crew members that would be responsible for managing the *Knight Discoverer* (KD). This crew would be transported to the moon for training. For them, it was a serious business, and everybody was taking every step seriously. Even in the middle of it all, Alexander's dream was coming true. He cherished science, and he loved using science to save humankind —something he was now lined up to do. It was only going to be a matter of time now, no more turning back!

Therefore, in the year 2133, the crew was lined up to go and complete the training and the final stages of the construction of the KD. Alexander and his people were scheduled to start the testing of all the equipment that was going to help them get to the 'Promised Land.'

Going back to Daisy, Alexander's mom, she was now old at this stage. Even though her age was well advanced now, the people around her and others not in her circles had great respect for her. They respected her because she was the ship designer. Her work of decades was finally going to help people escape problems that were compounding by each day on Earth —her ship would take them to *Canaan,* the promised land. Because of her works, her son thought it was natural that she was going to be coming with them to the moon for the final stages of the preparations, but he was to receive the shock of his life when he finally brings the subject up before her. Daisy was in her 50's when she gave birth to Alexander, and by now, she thought she was too old to take part in many things.

The *Knight Discoverer* had been built by the construction crew since 2110. The completion was expected to take 25 years due to the complexity of the project and all technological advances that needed to be implemented and invented to be placed inside such a revolutionary ship. There were just many things, or sciences that were to be included as each stage and every inch of the ship was to be carefully designed and strategically built to withstand the pressure that it would to go through when the time comes.

The ship needed to be very thin and stretched to support the spaghettification process inside the Sagittarius A Star. The amount of pressure that it was going to be going through was immense, hence the need to build it very thin. Alex and his crew understood all this, but instead of them getting anxious about getting things right, they were so excited about seeing their dreams come true. The outmost layer of the spaceship was also built to withstand the spaghettification process. No matter how thin the ship was going to appear, the passengers and crew would still be protected in the inside of the ship, right in the middle of it, so they would not suffer the consequences of the spaghettification process.

So, the crew finally left and found themselves landed on the Lunar Base Station. While here, many good things happened, including Alexander's first feeling of love in a very long time. This love was not the kind that he had for his mother, but the feeling of love for a girl, and indeed, it was a girl that his heart beat fast for. While at it, he was going to have to fight with others because the policy there was that no romantic relationships were to be allowed. But what the heart feels it what it wants.

Sofie was this confident young lady that showed excellence in many things pertaining to their job while on the moon. Besides her beauty, this quality of her also attracted Alexander's attention. She was very competent during their astronaut training sessions and earned Alex's respect. Even if she was good, Alex was excellent, and the two respected each other for that. They then first became friends, confidants, and, before they knew it, they had become lovers.

On the day they first spoke, Sofie was the one that approached Alexander during one of the breaks where people get a chance to talk about things away from work. "I hear your mom designed this." A sweet female voice spoke behind Alexander. He turned around and noticed that, for sure, the sweet voice was in tandem with the looks of the lady that owned it. She was slightly taller than him and had long hair that covered her small head. But even if her head was that small, it perfectly was a match for her big, blue eyes that looked like were borrowed from an angel. Because of her beauty, Alexander was stuck for a while and failed to respond to what she was saying. This did not usually happen to him. He was just a man devoted to his work, and for it to even happen when they were on this important mission was a miracle.

"Ahem," Alexander cleared his throat, trying to say something, but he was clearly stuck, and she jumped into his rescue.

"Sofie," she stretched out her hand to greet him as she said her name.

"Huh?" Alexander replied.

"Sofie, my name is Sofie. They call me Sofia back home, but you can call me Sofie." She smiled at him, and he looked like he was now getting back to the present moment.

"Alright, I see. I know you already. You are the girl trying to take my leading position on the crew. My name is Alexander."

"I know who you are, they all know you. And I am not trying to take anything away from you. I am just good at what I do." She winked at Alexander as she said this. Her beautiful smile seduced him, and he paused for a split second before responding to her. After he did, their conversation turned funny and comfortable for Alexander, leading to their friendship and romance in those months that followed.

Sofie was now in the habit of visiting Alexander in his chambers. On a particular visit, she decided to talk about the pictures that were by Alex's bed. The man was happy to talk about this since he had so much love for his Silva family, both the living and the dead.

"Over there is my family, my science, and my faith." He said

"How do you combine science and faith? Aren't they against one another?" Sofie asked.

"On the contrary. They complement each other. They are part of the same world. What science can't explain; faith helps me understand." Alexander said, before continuing, "I'll show you something."

He got the bible and started reading from the Book of Genesis Chapter 1 from verse 1 all the way to 27. After reading, he looked back at Sofie and said,

"The bible was written thousands of years ago. The book of Genesis is actually talking about the evolution of Our Universe. In the beginning was nothing, and from nothing, everything was created. Light was created. That's the Big Bang. The beginning of everything. The First stars and constellations were created, the first solar systems, Earth was created.

"Like in Genesis, life started in the ocean, and from the ocean, it went on to dry land and animals, from the land, Men and Women were created. You see, the science of evolution and the history in genesis complement each other. Now I ask you, Sofie. How come The Bible that was written thousands of years ago describes so perfectly the evolution of our universe and the life on Earth?" He was looking intently into her eyes. She couldn't stop smiling as she responded.

"I don't know." Sofie replied.

Alexander said, "I don't know either, but my faith tells me that God inspired us to write The Bible and to tell His History. The History of His Creation. The Creation of the Universe and US. He is giving us a second chance to find a new home for the whole humankind."

Alex also pointed out a picture that he had on the wall of his bedroom. It was a picture of a Poem written by a famous 20th Century Astronomer named Carl Sagan. This poem is called "The Pale Blue Dot." Alexander tells Sofie that he loves this poem because it describes how fragile Earth is in the immense emptiness of Space, and how much humans have misbehaved to make this Pale Blue Dot unable to sustain their own lives. Alexander tells Sofie that he hopes that *Canaan* will be a new chance for a new beginning for Humankind. A place that we should cherish each other and the planet that we live in.

After saying those words, they cuddled into a small hip and drowned in romance. After a while, Sofie discovered that she was pregnant. The two agreed that they could not let anyone know about this because romantic relationships on the Lunar Base station were not allowed altogether. They were to keep this secret until they cross over to the other side – *Canaan*. The launch of the Space Mission was just about to happen.

CHAPTER TEN
THE JOURNEY

Alexander and his people were scheduled to start testing all the equipment to help them get to the "Promised Land." As the ship's various instruments howled and sprang to life, eager to embark on the journey to humanity's future, Alexander couldn't help but reminisce, and soon he began to immerse himself within the glowing memory of his mother. Her work of decades was finally going to help people escape the prison they crafted on Earth. Her ship would take them to *Canaan,* her beliefs would usher in a new hope for humanity, she would bring all of mankind the hope that she had given to Alexander so many years ago. That hope pushed him to reach for the stars and be the man he needed to be when dire times fell upon him, and soon all his crewmates would feel the same as if they were within the clutches of a guardian angel, the *Knight Discoverer.*

Because of her work, her son thought it was natural that she would be coming with them to the Moon for the final stages of the preparations.

"What tremendous honor it would be to be a part of your life's first and final mission?" Alexander thought. "Surely, she would love to be with her family as we look for a better tomorrow?"

Amidst all the chaos on the surface of Earth, he had little time to wonder about such things, to dream about the future life he would hold and cherish; all he and his mother knew was the ash-ridden and scarred husk of their own dying world.

"Would things be different? Could things be better?

How will my grandchildren see our history?" So many thoughts with no accurate answers erupted into Alexander's mind.

Amidst his thoughts, the transport shuttle roared with flames during its test run breaking him out of his trance; the ideas eroded away as he found himself resolute and back to ensure his future.

With the Lunar Base Station completed, the team's stay was over, and their next stop was to back to Earth to enjoy the final moments among family and friends. The trip became smoother now, as though the burden of results was absent for the first time in a long while from Alexander's mind, he finally could take respite from the life of crisis that has possessed his life. Upon landing, Alexander saw he got his needs in order; many of his crewmates would go off to enjoy other earthly pleasures, living those few days like they were their last alive, but not Alexander. So, for his remaining hours, he chose a quiet respite, one with his mother.

Alexander looked out his window as he drove through Virginia; what the history books described as a fertile green land complete with rivers and forest all around has now become a shadow of itself. Trees were darkened and leafless; the waterways now cracked dried canyons devoid of life. Too many who lived before him destroyed the once breath-taking scenery; now, Alexander only had the images from videos to believe in.

"Was he worthy of going to the stars and find peace in a new Eden?" Alex's thoughts shooting like pistons.

Yet again, he was tormented by these inadequacies, taunted by himself as though he felt unworthy of helming the great expedition into the unknown, that he wasn't worthy of any of it. Perhaps his destiny was to remain here, with all those who will be abandoned once the shuttle leaves them behind.

"Perhaps they are blessed to end the cycle here?" Alexander thought.

Suddenly he broke his inner senses and turned left into the now brown, dust-filled land his home resided on. Alex turned off the ignition and went inside to see his mother.

Alexander looked to the sky; by now, it was dark; he then gazed toward the Moon base. He wondered how Sofie was spending these final hours, perhaps surrounded by family and friends. Maybe safe and sound alone dreaming of our soon-to-be child. He imagined how life would be for them and their upcoming baby while in *Canaan*, how magical it would be, him and his mother, soon to be wife and child, all together and safe from imminent doom. On this day, the last shuttle was supposed to leave Earth with the previous group of selectees. He remembered the route clearly. First liftoff, then the Moonbase, finally the wormhole, and perhaps peaceful *Canaan*, it's all said and done. All of them together, away from this mess.

After some moments, Alex began walking to go and talk to his mother to hear how she was feeling about the upcoming trip to the Moon and then to *Canaan*. He opened the door to the familiar warmth of home; despite what permeated the air around him, this still felt true; it felt suitable and cozy. Alexander's troubled thoughts immediately evaporated after a brief pause in the rustic ambiance of the building, and as soon as they leave, he sees his mother awaiting his arrival.

"Hi, mom, time to go to the ship. I hope you are ready, and all pumped up for the mission!" He bellowed with overflowing joy.

Daisy remained quiet; his mother was nowhere near ready to leave the house. Nothing was packed, her house was clean as a whistle, and everything was in the exact order as it had been before he left.

"What's going on here? She must have been ready by now; why hasn't she said anything?" he thought to himself.

Daisy interrupts Alexander's thoughts and directs him with a wave like when he was younger.

"I'm not going anywhere, son." She reluctantly responded, facing downwards as her white hair was the only thing Alexander could clearly see from his standing position.

"But Mama, that's your ship! You designed and built it! I don't understand?" His face looked worried.

"My work is done, son." she pauses to catch her breath, eventually wheezing out the last thing Alexander wanted to hear

"I'm not going. . ." This time again, her response was short, and she showed nothing would change her mind. Instead, she looked up at her son and continued talking. Her hair parted, and her wrinkled face now shown plainly to him.

"You know, I never told you this. But the same day I discovered I was expecting you, one of the missing drones from Carr sent us data that it had found a planet habitable by humans."

Daisy curls into her chair, coughing and catching her breath, eventually regaining her poise.

"It had found *Canaan*. That gave me hope, and that is why I named you Alexander. Do you know what your name means?"

"Does It mean I am your son?" Alexander replied sheepishly

Daisy smiled a weak smile and let out a laugh as quiet as a mouse. No less satisfied with her son's humor.

Daisy regained her composure, "That too," with a smile on her face, she said, "But it also means: "The Savior of Men." And here you are, the Commander of the *Knight Discoverer*, the last hope of mankind, the last hope of avoiding our extinction." She continued, feeling so much pride for her son. She was, indeed, satisfied with the work he was doing to complete a mission she started some decades ago.

She continued talking, "Do you think ALL of this is just a coincidence? This is God's Plan. You were born for this mission and for this purpose. Do you believe this?"

He answered, "I do, mother. I will not disappoint you."

Daisy lets out another ring of coughs and groans, trying to smile through the torrent of pain

Daisy said to Alexander, "I know you won't, you never did. . ."

Daisy pauses, this time resolute and filled with determination.

"We can talk about all the theories of the cosmos, all the mathematical equations to explain the universe and science, but do you know the thing that sums up the whole universe?" She asked Alex.

Alexander replied, "I don't."

Daisy whispers, "Love, my son. Love is the fundamental force that moves the universe and everything on it. It connects everything to it. It is more powerful than any force and faster than light. My love for you is infinite and eternal. It does not matter how far you are or where you are, my love for you will ALWAYS connect us, and God is Love."

Alexander knew his mother very well. If her mind is made up to do something, there was no way anyone would change her. He used to thank God that most of her thoughts were for the good of the people. Even if she were to be knuckle-headed about it, people would still benefit and not suffer out of her actions. He knew she was never going to change her mind. He drew closer to her, she stood up, and the two embraced each other and wept upon one another. It was not an easy thing for him to give his mother up for the last time. And for her, it wasn't easy to watch her son's back vanish into the heat of the day. Even though she was ready for this day, she still felt something huge had been plucked out of her life. As if a star had finally exploded and dispersed its energy throughout the cosmos.

Alex stood confident in front of his mother, but as the car started and he backed out of the driveway one last time, he wept. Not tears of solemn sorrow, but of genuine pride. If his mother could brave the threats put upon her, he must do the same.

His mother may have chosen her path, but he knew deep down she was right. Her love for him holds no boundaries; the same applied to her; no matter where he was or what he was doing, he would know she was there; a piece of her moved in every action he took. While his perfect future may not come to pass, he is confident that he may find peace still, much like his mother has. No matter what he faces, Sofie belonged with him, and Daisy's memories were etched in his heart forever. As the night eclipsed into a daylight shade, the climb to *Knight Discoverer* neared its beginning.

The time for Alexander and the last crew members to go to the Moon finally arrived. Everybody was ready to go there. As for Alexander and a few others who had been to the Moon once were more like business as usual, but for the ordinary people selected to go and help with colonizing *Canaan,* it was a dream come true, a new chance at a new life. They were so ecstatic about the mission. If they made it to *Canaan,* it surely would be a double celebration with the captain and his crew. For Alexander, he knew these people were his newfound responsibility, and he would ensure they made it to their new home, one way or another.

When the shuttle was ready to embark on the journey, everybody was asked to sit tight and firmly strap themselves in. Once everything was set in motion, distant spectators could see the shuttle spewing a blue flame around it. After a few seconds of the flame, it rapidly took off and slowly disappeared into the sky. Leaving them with smiles and tears of joy that their people were finally going to discover life in a better world. Alex looked outwards to the earth's horizon one final time and stood in silence.

CHAPTER ELEVEN
DECISIONS

The shuttles successfully took the crew and other people from Earth, finding themselves on the Moon. Once they arrived, many took it upon themselves to survey the Moon base and take one last glimpse upon their old home. Standing on the dome entrance, Alexander took a deep breath of the produced oxygen and prepared himself for his role as captain. He marched onto the landing bay and began to give a speech to the passengers

"Future settlers of *Canaan*," he bellowed, "Today, we mark the first step of our journey into the infinite! This Moon base is the last bit of home you will see for the rest of your natural lives, make sure to spend it wisely. We carry humanity's future to *Canaan*, and the light of our forefathers shine upon each one of us today."

Alexander takes a moment to contemplate, his mother's final words ringing through him like an empty stadium

"You have three hours to do all things you must before our journey continues; report back here once you're ready to depart." Alexander then waved at the passengers as many exited the station with PES systems, ready to explore the station.

"Does anyone have any questions to ask?" Alexander shouted at the top of his voice. All the remaining people stood silent. It seemed as if they had understood what their leaders were telling them all along. But, on the other hand, it seemed as if their silence was a confirmation reality began sitting in their minds.

Alexander took it upon himself to go with some of the passengers as well, he had roamed the station before, but this time felt more surreal than before. He equipped his gear and shambled out onto the firm Moon once again. Breathe in, breathe out, he kept repeating to himself as he wandered to a ledge near the base of the station's exit. Below him stood a cavern, stretched to the Moon's deepest core, an abyss of pitch-black darkness. He looked upwards towards the heavenly scene of planet Earth. He pictured how it used to look, shimmering blue waterways and green-filled masses with a beautiful beige underside making the whole vista genuinely breathtaking.

"Captain?" a voice announced over his signal "behind you, sir," he spoke again.

Alexander turned, and before him was a woman who he had never seen before.

"The view is something, ain't it?"

"Definitely nothing even close to the movies," Alexander responded.

The woman chuckled harder than he had ever seen someone laugh.

"You ever thought we'd see her like this? The whole thing is so huge and perfect?" the woman said

"Not exactly like this . . ." Alex uncomfortably murmured

"I've been up here a while captain, I've gotten to see this view dozens of times, and every time I think to myself what *Canaan* may look like. Will it be bluer than the sea? Brighter than the sun? What is it like to sit there like this? All things I can't wait to find out." the woman pauses for a second, then begins again

"Every time I look at the earth, I see the sun, and every time I see the sun, I feel the Moon, and I think about a book, Living with the Stars, you ever hear of it?"

Alexander shifts, knowing the text very well. He nods affirmingly.

"Do you really think that's true?" she inquires.

"Think what's true?"

"Do you think we're all made of stardust? I know it's a dumb question . . . but I always thought that was a cool idea. That humanity is just a bunch of destroyed stars that have the right components to make us. To think we are all connected the planets, the sun, *Canaan,* and us." The woman breaks off from her rant and looks inquisitively at her captain.

Alex responds, "I find it sweet, the idea that all energy comes from one thing, and we're all here because of it. It makes me feel like I have a purpose like I have a duty bigger than my own. Most of my life I've felt that way, but I never thought about that text in that way . . ."

He waits to collect his thoughts, but before he can speak, the woman stands, "Well, sir, sorry to disturb you, best be getting back to the ship, gotta take inventory."

The woman begins to move back to the ship but looks back at Alex and asks, "Do you really think we'll make it to *Canaan*?"

Alex stands as well, and with a nod of confidence, he replies "We will"

The woman smiled and returned to the ship, Alex following close behind; eventually, they made it back to the vessel.

Alexander was the Commander of the ship, and Sofie his First Officer. The two were determined to make history together as they prepared to lead the people from the Moon station to *Canaan*. Everybody was strapped up, ready to explore the new planet.

"You ready to roll, boy?" Sofie turned toward Alexander as she winked at him. "Oh, yes, we are doing this. And you know what it means, right?"

"What does it mean?" She asked him back.

He responded, "It means we get to raise our baby on the new planet!"

He sounded very excited as he lowered his voice so people around them wouldn't hear about the pregnancy. Sofie responded by giving him the warmest smile he had ever seen.

"But is everything OK with the engines?" Alex asked.

Sofie holds Alexander's hand firmly and stares into his eyes, and he into hers.

"Yes, relax, we are good to go, and all will be well. I know you want to make your mom proud, and today you are doing this. I am glad to be by your side as you accomplish this."

"But you are also doing this, Sofie."

"Come on, Alex, you know what I mean. Now, come on in, we got to go." This was going to be the best day for the people on this ship. They were finally getting on the road to escape the horrors of the life they once lived and ready to embrace brand new ones.

The *Knight Discoverer*, made thin to withstand pressure, made considerable noise as it prepared to take off. People inside kept quiet for a while as they looked like scared children while their bodies were strapped up on the ship's metallic walls. They held on tight to the side of their spacesuits. Everybody was deathly silent and looked like soldiers at the back of a cargo plane just waiting on instructions to take a parachute jump. The vessel whirred and screeched as the thrusters exploded with a bolt of force throughout the station. The K.D. stretched upwards into the ever-consuming space, and soon they found themselves going away from the Moon in the famous K.D. toward the great dark beyond.

For Alexander, the journey was necessary, and even though he had Sofie to keep on talking to, Sofie was his first immediate assistant; she wouldn't be there just for him, and he wouldn't be there just for her, the lives of everyone on board took precedence. So, the two made an outstanding team with love and care for the others on board.

As they transcended further into space, Daisy begins to cough profusely.

"Miss, are you alright" her caretaker exclaimed.

Daisy ceased her episode and responded with a voice akin to that of a sputtering car engine.

"I'm fine . . ." she paused for a moment then asked a question.

"Take me outside . . . I want to see my son make it to our new home." she collapsed as she tried to stand by herself.

"Daisy!" her caretaker exclaimed. "Let me get you up, Miss, you cannot get up; let me help you."

"No!" Daisy shouted. "I will go outside, I will see that ship, I will wave goodbye to my son."

Both women ceased speaking as her caretaker knew Daisy was serious. "Okay, Miss, I will help you see him."

Daisy buckles under the world's weight but needed help to get up to the porch. She sits down on her old rocking chair and feels the harsh breeze of warm dusty air perforate her face. Then, she sees the light of the shuttle zipping towards the wormhole.

Back in the shuttle, Alex and Sofie continue their banter as usual. Suddenly a robotic voice cries out from the intercom. "Engine room malfunction, ionic engine compromised, requires manual instantiation."

Panic arose within Alex's heart; he knew calamity was mere minutes away. An ionic engine overload is the last thing they needed from this mission, one faulty excess and the engine could return the ship's integrity by the atom; this was the same problem that had happened with the failed Allen probe, and Alex wasn't going to let that happen again. Alex stood tall and collected, prepared to sprint toward the engine room; no passenger would be spared from the coming explosion.

Alex's choices are grim. If he cannot fix this problem, humanity's hope dies, his legacy dies with him, and his mother will surely die alone and heartbroken.

Alex turns to Sofie. "Sofie, keep yourself safe and keep everyone on board safe. That engine is going to blow unless someone manually defuses it."

Sofie turns to him as well and speaks curtly, "No! You don't have to do this; there must be another way, another option, you can't leave me! Don't die like a hero! I need you!" she begins to try to hold him back from pursuing the reactor.

Alex thinks back to his mother, father, and all the many things that kept him anchored to the earth. He remembers what it may be like on *Canaan*; all things are connected. He remembers the woman on the Moon, her vast-eyed excitement at how much more life could be, how we are all connected, how we are all a part of each other. Of course, the ionic engine will be dangerous, but what would his mother do in the face of disarray and chaos?

She wouldn't back down, and neither will he. "And I am not ready to lose myself as I lose you too in the process. Hold on to this. I love you and our unborn child. My love for you is forever. I will always be with you," he concluded as he handed his necklace to Sofie.

With shaking hands, she took hold of it with one hand as the other tried to hold Alexander's hand. He quickly looked away as he made his way into the ionic engine room. Before entering the room, he said his prayer

"Give me the wisdom and knowledge I need to make this decision. Make me follow your will. Amen."

With his mind transparent and his purpose clearer, he stepped foot into the jaws of the beast.

Sofie watched him walk into this room. She thought if his mother had come with them, she would have been able to stop him. But she did not know this would not have made a difference because of Alexander's love for people and the fact his mother was sick and seated outside her house, just imagining that his son was somewhere up there trying to save the world.

The door slammed shut as Alex's screaming and the shuttles rumbling became apparent to all the passengers.

The engine room was a sphere like a deathtrap; ionic expulsions blazed from the engine rapidly, with the matter it contacted being discharged through every atom. On an atomic level, the items would fade away like ash in the wind. As he was stretching his arms wide open and trying to balance himself on top of a beam inside the Ionic Engine, he saw the bracelet that her mom gave to him with the words 'God's blessings and hard work' inscribed within the mineral. Seeing that prompted him to whisper, "This is for you, mom." It sure sounded like his last words as he gathered all the courage that was in him. He ran to the discharge station with great haste and pulled the lever; as the crank fell, so too did he, as the engine spewed out a torrent of death within the hold, the rest of Alex was no more, but dust in the wind and a bracelet swept away within the compartment. Finally, the engine fell dormant, and the wormhole encompassed the ship.

On Earth, Daisy was still waiting for the sunrise when the burst of light coming from the ionic engine hit Alexander. As it happened, this became the first burst of sunlight hit Daisy's eyes; she felt a force, something ruptured through her as though a part of her was wiped from memory, eradicated from existence. She felt lighter than air but heavier than steel all at once. Then, in many years, Daisy stood up successfully for once and spoke, "God's blessings and hard work."

She stood triumphantly for the last time then and soon collapsed to the porch, this time as a flame snuffed out by the wind. Forever dormant. Two lives were claimed and soon returned to space, where they were once born from and soon will be born again.

While watching this happening, Sofie stood there with her mouth wide open and right hand over her belly. She did not know what to say as her newly found lover just decided to sacrifice his life for those aboard the ship. The crew was aghast at the sight and sounds of the dead captain, but Sofie looked at his last gift. Sofie stood tall and spoke, "Look, lively colonists! Our future is almost here!" she stood firm as they looked upon her. Emboldened by Alex's words and steadfast in her resolve. She stood there, ready for the space jump. Alexander was a courageous man. He would have continued with the mission and then mourned later when everybody else was safe.

Dealing with her grief, Sofie was coming toward the wormhole, prepared for the space jump, and *Knight Discoverer* was about to enter Sagittarius. Sofie stared in awe at the wormhole, a black opening in which light could not escape; nothing could escape. They entered the wormhole, and the ship was performing as expected. The spaghettification process had commenced, and the outermost layer of KD was being compressed and stretched. Meanwhile, the living quarters were well protected. The passengers screamed and wailed, sounds distorted and in disarray. Matter itself seemed inconclusive as though reality bent to the black hole, and all within its grasp were along for the experience. Soon the horrific entry was finished as they sped through the Inner Event Horizon. Dazzling lights like the rays of many suns burst through the shuttle's windows, colors beyond the comprehension danced within the ship's inner hull as they blended to become mixtures of spectacular images, like fireworks from Heaven.

The light then erupted into a spew of bending matter; as their exit was closer and closer, the light refracted upon itself and established a dazzling show of beauty that seemed to bleed from the walls themselves. The matter seemed to morph between forms on a microscopic level within mere seconds, as chairs and various items were liquefied and erupted into solid expulsion. Then, upon the lights exiting their view, it was over. A new solar system awaited them in space. The cabin erupted in joy and wonder as they saw the planet soon to be their home, all except Sofie.

CHAPTER TWELVE
CANAAN

The ship landed on the fresh soil of *Canaan,* its thrusters now silent and its landing deck now opened. It was a dream comes true for all the people in it – perhaps only Sofie felt bewildered. But, nevertheless, she had to remain courageous until the mission was completed.

She had gathered her courage and successfully led the rest of the people through space, and even more so through a black hole, a feat no human could claim before her. Because of that, she knew she could do it again; now, the people needed leadership again to complete the mission to the soils of *Canaan*. Sofie did not believe it when the monitor showed a new planet; they had never set foot on. Seeing it there sent the whole team and some passengers into delirium. Their quick and fiery celebration as they realized they would be allowed to have families and live on proper soil, with adequate water, and a world that was as alive and breathing as they were.

Landing there was greeted only by sites of beauty. *Canaan* was a beautiful planet composed of gargantuan hills and deep valleys, mountain peaks, and deep flowing rivers, everything they could have ever dreamed of. The atmosphere there was breathable for humans, and they felt the difference, a far cry for people running away from polluted air. The planet was exuberant with natural beauties, reminding them of the Earth when it was still in its best days – before human activity ransacked the many wonders of the world. It seemed like a paradise given by God, a new beginning for humanity. As they looked at this newfound land, they could only hope they would take better care of this new Eden.

After discovering the challenge waiting for them, the people decided to pitch tents in a nearby area as they went to sleep. The night came swiftly after their landing, and the Moon filled the night sky with a dazzling spectacle of stars and celestial bodies all around. A sight so pure and breathtaking, many of the new inhabitants found rest could not just come easily. Many of them could be heard twisting and turning throughout the night after the long voyage. Those who chose to celebrate with more sensual activities saw this as an opportunity to delight themselves with acts of passion with their loved ones. Who would blame them? They were in a new area; no one really knew what would befall them the following day. The new colony of humanity ensured its first breathtaking night was one they would not forget.

The next day came, and it gave Sofie's crew a chance to begin a new day in this place. They were delighted to see that the sun rose just as it did on earth, almost as if the planets were mirror images of each other, too perfect to be accurate, and yet it was. The cycle of the day went as expected, hours passed, and the colonists began to explore and settle in; many found various creatures unseen by normal human eyes before, towering beasts and tiny critters darted the planet's trees and valleys. Flora and fauna thrived here, everywhere to be seen. It was akin to that of paradise. Many settlers broke off into irrigation parties, and others established a setup for their first structures in the world. Much more spread out into the far reaches of the plain they landed upon, hoping to discover new things with each step. Everyone went to feel like they were in heaven, all except Sofie.

The sun began its descent into the horizon, marking the end of the first actual day for the settlers and for Sofie. This was the first sunset in *Canaan,* and she wished to experience it alone, in total awe of the majestic journey she had almost completed. While looking at the beautiful two-star sunset from JSA and AFDATA stars, both fading behind the evergreen landscape, she grabbed Alexander's necklace and put her hands over her womb. She felt hope again. Hope that Mankind would learn its lessons this time and be gentler and wiser with this new home. She thought about her child's future, watching the stars etch their final ray of energy across the skies of *Canaan*; Sofie makes her way to her feet and walks away from the cliff into the warming campfires joyous laughter of her new family. She smiles and walks into the blazing light, with pride and poise, ready for what tomorrow may bring.

BOOK REVIEW

Filho and Alencar's fast-moving tale cites sources ranging from Einstein and Carl Sagan to the book of Genesis (and it seems fair to toss the 2014 movie Interstellar in there, too). The language of the narrative is related in a colloquial style more akin to a lecture hall than a brick thick, hard–SF tome: "But like we mentioned in the previous chapter, these kinds of developments take ample time to bring to completion. No one really wants to produce something that takes that amount of knowledge and time only for it to falter in the end. This is the same thing as what happened in the previous chapter with Joseph and Daisy." While there are some mind-stretching digressions into spacetime and quantum entanglement, the simplified plotting and (largely) nontechnical prose make the enjoyable volume suitable for the YA and middle-grade readerships of any planet.

—KIRKUS REVIEWS

www.ingramcontent.com/pod-product-compliance
Lightning Source LLC
LaVergne TN
LVHW050135080526
838202LV00061B/6493